Lois A. Fison, Walter Thomas

Merry Suffolk - Master Archie and Other Tales

Lois A. Fison, Walter Thomas

Merry Suffolk - Master Archie and Other Tales

ISBN/EAN: 9783744786133

Printed in Europe, USA, Canada, Australia, Japan

Cover: Foto ©Andreas Hilbeck / pixelio.de

More available books at **www.hansebooks.com**

MERRY SUFFOLK

MASTER ARCHIE AND OTHER TALES

A Book of Folk=Lore

By LOIS A. FISON

Author of " Brother Mike " & " New Fairy Land ;"

WITH WHICH IS INCLUDED

'TOM TIT TOT" AND SEQUEL

By MRS. WALTER THOMAS

" You'll ha' to spin five skeins a dar "

LONDON

JARROLD & SONS, 10 & 11, WARWICK LANE, E.C.

[*All Rights Reserved*]

1899

PREFACE.

THE Folk-Lore in these pages has been collected from Suffolk Folk, and connected by the aid of stories.

The Suffolk Sayings and Riddles have the same origin, and the Author has purposely not given the Suffolk dialect correctly broad from pity to those who do not understand it.

In "The Bookman" for October, 1893 (page 21), Mr. Francis Groom wrote :—" Suffolk has the distinction of having produced by far the best versions of the old *Folk Lore* hitherto collected in England." They are three only in number—'Cap o' Rushes,' 'Tom Tit Tot,' and 'Brother Mike.'* They were contributed to a set of 'Suffolk Notes and Queries,' that I edited sixteen years ago for the *Ipswich Journal.* They are now being republished in an illustrated form by the Collectors, Mrs. Walter Thomas and Miss L. A. Fison, to whom as children they were told by their old nurse.

The Author is indebted to Mr. H. F. Euren and Mr. William Jarrold (who published the charming story, " Brother Mike," showing his knowledge and love of true Folk-Lore), for an introduction to Mr. William Bottrell's " Traditions and Heath-side Stories of West Cornwall," printed in 1875, where a

* " Brother Mike " has already appeared.

s.ory will be found called "Duffy and the Devil." Here the family likeness to the old German Folk Story of "Tom Tit Tot" is plainly seen. The tale was given as a Christmas Play in Cornwall formerly.

We find here told, that a rich Squire, "Lovel," marries Duffy because he hears she is the best spinster and knitster in the county. By aid of an old witch, the girl Duffy gets the help of a devil called "Buck-a-boo," who spins for her, but demands as his reward that she shall marry him at the end of three years unless she can tell his name.

The Squire when hunting sees a band of witches dancing in a wood with "Buck-a-boo" their master. The witches sing,

> " By night and by day,
>   We will dance and play,
> With our noble captain,
>   ' Farraway,' ' Farraway.' "

Duffy finds the name therefore, when the Squire tells her what he has seen, and when the devil comes to carry Duffy away, she astonishes him by saying his name, and so escapes, as the Queen does in "Tom Tit Tot."

And in the second part or Sequel of this Tale, the heroine escapes from danger through the aid of the Wise Woman, much as the Queen in "Tom Tit Tot" does by the help of the Gipsies.

The Author begs to express sincere thanks to the friends who have kindly given her most valuable assistance in her work, especially to Mr. Francis Groom, Professor Cowell, and others, who have sent her old Suffolk Sayings, etc.

CONTENTS.

MERRY SUFFOLK.

TOM TIT TOT.

THE SUFFOLK VERSION OF GRIMM'S TALE, "RUMPELSTILTSKIN."

WELL, once upon a time there were a woman, and she baked five pies, and when they come out on the oven, they was that overbaked the crust was too hard for to ate. Soo says she to her darter,

"Mawther," says she, "put them pies up on the shelf, du, and they'll soon come agin." (She meant the crust would get soft.)

Well, the gal set 'um on the shelf, and says she,

"Lork! if they pies 'll come agin, I'll ate 'um all now," says she.

Soo she set too work and eat 'um all, first and last, that she did.

Well, come supper-time the woman she said,

"Goo you and git one of them there pies. I daresay they've come agin now."

The gal she went, an' she looked, and there warn't nothin' but the dishes. So back she come and says she,

" Noo, they ain't come agin."

" Not none on 'em ? " says the mother.

" Not none on 'em," says she.

" Well, come agin or not come agin," says the woman, " I'll ha' one for supper."

" But you can't if they ain't come," says the gal.

" But I can," says she. " Goo you and bring the best of 'em."

" Best or worst," says the gal, " I've ate 'em all, and you can't ha' one till that's come agin."

Well, the woman she was wholly bate, and she took her spinnin' to the door to spin, and as she spun she sang,

> " My darter ha' ate five pies to-day
> My darter ha' ate five, five pies to-day."

The king he were a comin' down the street, an' he hard her sing, but what she sang he couldn't hare, so he stopped and said,

" What were that you was a singun of, maw'r ? "

The woman she were ashamed to let him hare what her darter had been a-doin', so she sang 'stids o' that :

> " My darter ha' spun five, five skeins to-day,
> My darter ha' spun five, five skeins to-day."

" S'ars o' mine! " said the king. " I never heerd tell of anyone as could do that."

Then he said, " Look you here, I want a wife, and I'll marry your darter. But look you here," says he, " 'leven months out o' the year she shall have all the vittles she likes to eat, and all the gownds she likes to git, and all the cump'ny she likes to hev, but the last month o' the year, she'll hev to spin five skeins iv'ry day, an' if she doon't, I shall kill her."

" All right," says the woman, for she thowt what a grand marriage that was. And as for them five skeins when te come tew, there'd be plenty o' ways of gettin' out of it, and, likeliest, he'd ha' forgot about it.

Well, so they was married. An' for 'leven months the gal had all the vittles she liked to ate, and all the gownds she liked to git, and all the cumpn'y she liked to hev. But when the time was gettin' oover, she began to think about them there skeins, an' to wonder if he had 'em in mind. But not one word did he say about 'em, an' she wholly thowt he'd forgot 'em.

Howsivir, the last day o' the last month he takes her to a room she'd nivir set eyes on afore. There wam't nothing in it but a spinnin' wheel and a stool. An' says he,

" Now, me dear, hare you'll be shut in to-morrow with some vittles and some flax, and if you ain't spun five skeins by the nights, yar hid 'll goo off."

An' awa' he went about his business. Well, she were that frightened. She'd allus been such a gatless mawther, that she didn't so much as know how to spin; an' what were she to dew to-morrer, with no one to come nigh her to help her? She sat down on a stool in the kitchen, and lork! how she did cry! Howsivir, all on a sudden she hard a sort of a knockin' low down on the door. She upped and oped it, an' what should she see but a small little black thing with a long tail, that looked up at her right kewrious, an' that said,

"What are you a-cryin' for?"

"What's that to yew?" says she.

"Never yew mind," that said. "But tell me what you're a-cryin' for."

"That oon't dew me noo good if I dew," says she.

"Yew doon't know that," that said, an' twirled that's tail round.

"Well," says she, "that oon't dew no harm, if that doon't dew no good," and she upped and told about the pies, an' the skeins an' everything.

"This is what I'll dew," says the little black thing, "I'll come to yar winder iv'ry mornin' an' take the flax, an' bring it spun at night."

"What's your pay?" says she.

That looked out o' the corners o' that's eyes, an' that said,

"I'll give you three guesses every night to guess my name,

an' if you hain't guessed it afore the month's up, yew shall be mine."

Well, she thowt she'd be sure to guess that's name afore the month was up.

"All right," says she; "I agree."

"All right," that says; and lork! how that twirled that's tail!

Well, the next day har husband he took her inter the room, an' there was the flax an' the day's vittles.

"Now, there's the flax," says he, "an' if that ain't spun up this night off goo yar hid."

An' then he went out an' locked the door. He'd hardly goon, when there was a knockin' agin the winder. She upped and she oped it, and there sure enough was the little oo'd thing a-settin' on the ledge.

"Where's the flax?" says he.

"Here te be," says she. An' she gonned it to him.

Well, come the evenin' a knockin' come agin the winder. She upped an' she oped it, and there were the little oo'd thing with five skeins o' flax on his arm.

"Here te be," says he. An' he gonned it to her.

"Now what's my name?" says he.

"What is that Bill?" says she.

"Noo, that ain't," says he. An' he twirled his tail.

"Is that Ned?" says she.

" Noo, that ain't," says he.   An' he twirled his tail.

" Well is that Mark ? " says she.

" Noo, that ain't," says he.   An' he twirled his tail harder,
an' awa' he flew.

Well, when har husband he come in, there was the five
skeins riddy for him.

" I see I sharn't hev for to kill yew to-night, my dare," says
he.   " Yew'll hev yar vittles an' yar flax in the morning," says
he, an' awa' he goes.

" Well, ivery day the flax an' the vittles they was brought,
an' ivery day that there little black impet used for to come
mornin's and evenin's.   An' all the day the mawther she set
a-tryin' fur to think of names to say to it when te come at
night.   But she niver hot on the right one.   An' as that got
towarts the ind o' the month, the impet that began for to
look soo maliceful, an' that twirled that's tail faster an' faster
each time she gave a guess.   At last te came te the last day
but one.   The impet that come at night along o' the five
skeins, an' that said,

" What ! hain't yew got my name yet ? "

" Is that Nicademus ? " says she.

" Noo, tain't," that says.

" Is that Sammle, " says she.

" Noo, tain't," says he.

" A-well, is that Methusalem ? " says she.

" Noo, tain't that norther," he says.

Then that looks at her with that's eyes like a cool o' fire, an' that says,

" Woman, there's only to-morrer night, an' then yar'll be mine." An' awa' he flew.

Well, she felt that horrud. Howsomediver, she hard the king a-comin' along the passage. In he came, an' when he see the five skeins he says, says he,

" Well, me dare," says he, " I don't see but what yew'll ha' your skeins ready to-morrer night as well, an' as I reckon I shorn't ha' to kill you, I'll ha' supper in here to-night."

So they brought supper, an' another stool for him, and down the tew they sat.

Well, he hadn't eat but a mouthful or so, when he stops, an' begins to laugh.

" What is it ? " says she.

" A-why," says he, " I was out a-huntin' to-day, an' I got away to a place in the wood I'd never seen afore. An' there was an old chalk pit. An' I heerd a sort of a hummin', kind o'. So I got off my hobby an' I looked down. Well, what should there be but the funniest little black thing yew iver set eyes on. An' what was that a-dewin' on, but that had a little spinnin' wheel, an' that were a-spinnin' wonful fast, an' a twirlin' that's tail. An' as that span, that sang,

> " Nimmy, nimmy not,
>   My name's Tom Tit Tot."

Well, when the mawther heerd this, she fared as if she could ha' jumped outer her skin for joy, but she din't say a word.   .

Next day that there little thing looked soo maliceful when he come foo the flax.   An' when the night came, she hurd that a-knockin' agin the winder panes.   She oped the winder, an' that come right in on the ledge.   That were grinnin' from are to are, an' o-o ! that's tail were twirlin' round so fast.

" What's my name? " that says, as that gonned the skeins.

" Is that Solomon ? " she says, pretendin' to be afeard.

" Noo, it ain't," that says, an' that come fudder inter the room.

" Well, is that Zebedee ? " says she agin.

" Noo, tain't," says the impet.   An' then that laughed an' twirled that's tail, till yew cou'n't hardly see it.

" Take time, woman," that says; " next guess an' you're mine."   An' that stretched out that's black hands at her.

Well, she backed a step or two, an' she looked at it, and then she laughed out, an' says she, a-pointin' of her finger at it,

> " Nimmy, nimmy not,
>   Yar name's Tom Tit Tot."

Well, when that hard her, that shruck awful, an' awa' that flew into the dark, an' she niver saw it noo more.

Lork! how she did clap her hands for joy! " I'll warrant my master'll ha' forgot all about spinning next year," says she.

THE GIPSY WOMAN.

WELL, the hool o' that yare the mawther* she'd the best o' livin' an' the best o' cump'ny, till the 'leventh month was nare over.

An' then har husban' says to her, says he,

"Well, me dare, to-day that's the end o' the month, an' to-morrer you'll ha' to begin an' spin yar five skeins ivvery day."

She hadn't nivver given a thowt but what he'd clane forgotten about it, an' now what te dew she did not know. She knew she couldn't reckon noo moor on Tom Tit Tot, an' she couldn't spin a mite herself; an' now har hid 'ud hav to come off!

Well, pore toad, she set herself down agin on a stule in the back-house, an' she cried as if har heart 'ud break. All at onst, she hared someone a-knockin' at the door. Soo she

* "Mawther," Suffolk for girl.

upped an' onsnecked it, an' there stood a gipsy woman, as brown's a berry.

"Why, wha's this te-dew hare?" sez she. "What air yew a-cryin' for like that?"

"Git awa', yew golderin' mawther," says she.. "Doon't yew come where yew ain't noo good."

"Tell me yar trouble, an' may be I shall be some good," says the woman.

Well she looked soo onderstandin' that the queen she upped an' toold her.

"Wha's that all?" sez she. "I ha' hoped folks out o' wuss than this, an' I'll help yew out o' this."

"Ah, but what de yew arst for dewin' of it?" sez the queen, for she thowt how she'd nare gonned herself awa' to that snaisly little black impet.

"I doon't ask nothun' but the best suit o' clothes yew ha' got," the gipsy said.

"Yow shall hev 'em an' welcome," says the queen, an' she runned an' ooped the hutch where har best gownd an' things was, an' giv 'em to the woman, an' a brooch o' gay goold. For she thowt to herself, "If she's a chate, an' can't help me, an' my hid is cut off, that woon't make no matters, if I *hev* giv awa' my best gownd."

The woman she looked rarely plazed when she see the gown, an' sez she,

"Now, then, yow'll ha' to ask all the fooks yew know to a stammin' grand partery. An' I'll come tew it."

Well, the mawther she went to her husband, an' says she,

"My dare, being that 'tis the larst night afoor I spin, I should like to hev a partery."

"All right, me dare," sez he. Soo the fooks wuz all arst, an' they come in their best clothes: silks an' sattuns, an' all mander o' fine things. Well, they all had a grand supper o' the best o' vittles, an' they liked theirselves rarely well. But the gipsy woman she nivvir come nigh, an' the queen, har heart was in 'har mouth. One of the lords as was right tired o' dancin' said that worn't far from bull's noon, an' te wuz time te goo.

"Noo, noo, dew yew sta' a little longer," says the queen. "Le's hev a game o' blind man's buff fust."

So they began to play. Just then the door that flew open, an' in come the gipsy woman. She'd woished herself an' coomed har hair, an' whelmed a gay an' gah handkercher round har hid, an' put on the gran' gownd till she looked like the queen come in.

"S'ars o' mine, whu's that?" says the king.

"Oo, tha's a frind o' mine,' says the queen. An' she looked to see what the gipsy 'ud dew.

"What! are yew a-playin' blind man's buff?" sez she. "I'll jine in along o' ye."

An' soo she did. But in har pocket what wuz there but a little gotch of cold cart grease, an' as she run, she dipped har hand in this hare grease, an' smudged it on the fooks as she run by.

That wom't long afore somebody hollered out, " Oo, lork! there's some rare nasty stuff on my gownd! "

" Why, soo there is on mine," sez another. " That must ha' come off of yow."

" Noo, that that din't. Yew ha' put it on to me."

An' then nigh ivverybody began to holler an' quarrel with ache other, ache one a-thinkin' that the tother had gone an' smirched 'em.

Well, the king he come forrerd an' he heerd what was the matter. The ladies was a-cryin' an' the gentlemen was a-shouten', an' all their fine things was daubed over.

" Wha's this?" he sah, for there was a great mark on his coat-sleeve, an' says he,

" Why, that's cart grease! "

" Noo, that ain't," sez the gipsy woman. " That's off my hand. Tha's spindle grease."

" Why, wha's spindle grease?" sez he.

" Well, says she, " I ha' been a great spinner i' my time, an' I span an' span an' span five skeins a day. An' becos I span se much the spindle grease, that, worked inter my hands, and now woish 'em as often as I may, I naster everything I touch. An' if yar wife spins like I, she'll ha' spindle grease like I."

Well, the king he looked at his coat-sleeve, an' he rubbed it, an' then he said,

"Look yew hare, me dare, an' listen what I sa' to yew. If ivver I see yew with a spindle agin in yar hands, yar hid'll goo off."

An' tha's all.

Gathered from her old nurse by
Anna Walter Thomas.

*CAP O' RUSHES.

W ELL, there was once a very rich gentleman, and he'd three daughters. And he thought to see how fond they was of him. So he says to the first,

" How much do you love me, my dear?"

" Why," says she, " as I love my life."

" That's good," says he.

So he says to the second, " How much do *you* love me, my dear?"

" Why," says she, " better nor all the world."

" That's good," says he.

So he says to the third, " How much do *you* love me, my dear?"

" Why, I love you as fresh meat loves salt," says she.

Well, he were that angry. " You don't love me at all," says he, " and in my house you stay no more."

So he drove her out there and then, and shut the door in her face.

* Cap o' Rushes is a Suffolk Folk-Lore version of the " King Lear" story, closely approximating to the Scottish " Rastricoat " varient.

Well, she went away, on and on, till she came to a fen. And there she gathered a lot of rushes, and made them into a cloak, kind o', with a hood, to cover her from head to foot, and to hide her fine clothes. And then she went on and on till she came to a great house.

"Do you want a maid?" says she.

"No, we don't," says they.

"I haven't nowhere to go," says she, "and I'd ask no wages, and do any sort of work," says she.

"Well, says they, "if you like to wash the pots, and scrape the saucepans, you may stay," says they.

So she stayed there, and washed the pots, and scraped the saucepans, and did all the dirty work. And because she gave no name, they called her Cap o' Rushes.

Well, one day there was to be a great dance, a little way off, and the servants was let to go, and look at the grand people. Cap o' Rushes said she was too tired to go, so she stayed at home. But when they was gone she offed with her cap o' rushes, and cleaned herself, and went to the dance. And no one there was so finely dressed as her.

Well, who should be there but her master's son, and what should he do but fall in love with her the minute he set eyes on her. He wouldn't dance with anyone else.

But before the dance were done, Cap o' Rushes she slipped off, and away she went home. And when the other maids was back, she was framin' to be asleep with her cap o' rushes on.

Well, next morning they says to her, " You did miss a sight, Cap o' Rushes."

" What was that?" says she.

" Why, the beautifullest lady you ever see dressed right gay and ga'. The young master he never took his eyes off her."

" Well, I should ha' liked to have seen her," says Cap o' Rushes.

" Well, there's to be another dance this evening, and perhaps she'll be there."

But, come the evening, Cap o' Rushes said she was too tired to go with them. Howsumdever, when they was gone she offed with her cap o' rushes, and cleaned herself, and away she went to the dance.

The master's son had been reckoning on seeing her, and he danced with no one else, and never took his eyes off of her. But before the dance was over, she slipped off, and home she went, and when the maids came back she framed to be asleep with her cap o' rushes on.

Next day they says to her again, " Well, Cap o' Rushes, you should ha' been there to see the lady. There she was again gay and ga', and the young master he never took his eyes off her."

"Well, there," says she, "I should ha' liked to ha' seen her."

"Well," says they, "there's a dance again this evening, and you must go with us, for she's sure to be there."

Well, come the evening, Cap o' Rushes said she was too tired to go, and do what they would she stayed at home. But when they was gone, she offed with her cap o' rushes, and cleaned herself, and away she went to the dance.

The master's son was rarely glad when he see her. He danced with none but her, and never took his eyes off of her. When she wouldn't tell him her name, nor where she came from, he gave her a ring, and told her if he didn't see her again he should die.

Well, afore the dance was over, off she slipped, and home she went, and when the maids came home, she was framing to be asleep, with her cap o' rushes on.

Well, next day they says to her, "There, Cap o' Rushes, you didn't come last night, and now you won't see the lady, for there's no more dances."

"Well, I should rarely like to ha' seen her," says she.

The master's son he tried every way to find out where the lady was gone, but go where he might, and ask whom he might, he never heard nothing about her. And he got worse and worse for the love of her till he had to keep his bed.

"Make some gruel for the young master," they says to the cook. "He's dying for love o' the lady."

The cook she set about making it, when Cap o' Rushes came in.

"What are you a-doin' on?" says she.

"I'm going to make some gruel for the young master," says the cook, "for he's dying for love of the lady."

"Let me make it," says Cap o' Rushes.

Well, the cook wouldn't at first, but at last she said yes; and Cap o' Rushes made the gruel. And when she had made it, she slipped the ring into it on the sly, before the cook took it upstairs.

The young man he drank it, and he saw the ring at the bottom.

"Send for the cook," says he. So up she comes.

"Who made this here gruel?" says he.

"I did," says the cook, for she was frightened. And he looked at her.

"No, you didn't," says he. "Say who did it, and you shan't be harmed."

"Well, then, 'twas Cap o' Rushes," says she.

"Send Cap o' Rushes here," says he.

"Did you make the gruel?" says he.

"Yes, I did," says she.

"Where did you get this ring?" says he.

" From him as gave it me," says she.

" Who are you then?" says the young man.

" I'll show you," says she. And she offed with her cap o' rushes, and there she was in her beautiful clothes.

Well, the master's son he got well very soon, and they was to be married in a little time. It was to be a very grand wedding, and everyone was asked far and near.

And Cap o' Rushes' father was asked. But she never told nobody who she was. But afore ,the wedding she went to the cook, and says she,

" I want you to dress every dish without a mite o' salt."

" That'll be rarely nasty," says the cook.

" That don't signify," says she.

" Very well," says the cook.

Well, the wedding-day came, and they was married. And after they was married all the company sat down to their vittles.

When they began to eat the meat, that was so tasteless they couldn't eat it. But Cap o' Rushes' father he tried first one dish and then another, and then he burst out crying,

" What is the matter?" said the master's son to him.

" Oh!" says he, " I had a daughter, and I asked her how much she loved me, and she said, 'As much as fresh meat loves salt.' And I turned her from my door, for I thought she didn't love me.　And now I see she loved me best of all. And she may be dead for aught I know."

"No, father, here she is," says Cap o' Rushes.　And she goes up to him, and puts her arms round him.　And so they was happy ever after.

Gathered by Mrs. Walter Thomas.

MASTER ARCHIE.

HOME AGAIN TO *SELY SUFFOLK.

T HE village of Beechwood is well known as the most
charming of all the pretty villages in Central Suffolk.
Its people keep up the character of "Merry England," and
in their joyous voices you hear the dialect of Suffolk com-
pletely unchanged.

There you see the finest oaks in the county, and its noble
cedars are unrivalled in size; their age is a great subject of
dispute among the people, some even declaring that King
Alfred planted them, and some that there was a tale about
"the brave queen what fought along o' them Romans, an'
bet 'um one time, but then she were bet. An' how when she
consated they Romans was a-going to ketch a hode on her,

* Sely—joyful, happy.—*Chaucer.*

NOTE.—It is hoped that lovers of Suffolk will pardon the dialect not being
given broad, but smoothed down out of pity to those who do not understand it.

why she druv as hard as ever she could, an' cum to they Beechwood Cedars, she did, an' under they she hid herself, an' when she heard the soldiers a-comin' after her there, why she took an' drunk pison, an' died afore they ever got nigh where she lar."

" They du saa as folks used to hear o' dark nights, hosses a-prancing round they owd trees—that wus years ago; the oud men sar they heard as much from their grandfathers, an' as how the min on the hosses han't no hids, nor yet the ode hosses nather."

But the old men are dead who told this story; we cannot hear more about it, and must be content to look with wonder at the old-world trees, and dream of the legends, as we sit under the sweeping branches of the cedars in the twilight of their shade.

The fine old hall of Beechwood is a perfect picture of beauty, with the river flowing past, reflecting its handsome Elizabethan front, and the trees of the woods rising behind, forming a background to the whole.

Sir Archibald Beechwood was one of the real old gentlemen of past days. He was beloved by all for his wise kindness, and in days when there was a growing dissatisfaction in the country between the landlord and tenants, he never had any trouble to keep the peace. At the time we write, Lady Beechwood was dead, and Sir Archibald and his eldest son, Hugh, were the only dwellers at the hall. All was very different there now to the merry life of former days. For now none of his family were left to Sir Archibald but the eldest son, and Archibald, or Archie (as all called him), who was with his regiment in India. How all in the village longed for the return of the handsome young soldier, who was a great favourite among rich and poor! He made himself one of the people, going in and out among their cottages, and delighting to study his favourite Suffolk dialect, in which he became as perfect as any of them, and had the utmost horror of its ever dying out.

But now the favourite " Archie" shall speak for himself.

I had been many years away from my old Suffolk home, but each year seemed to make my love stronger, and the longing for home less endurable. How welcome our east winds would have been in India! Why had I ever abused those very refreshing gusts? How I longed for Beechwood again, for the old hall, with its dear inmates, for my dear old friends in the village; to hear them speak to me in their gladsome voices, but, alas! a great fear has come over me, for I am told that the delightful dialect I loved so well has been swept away by Board School teaching. Perhaps I should never hear again the real Suffolk voice, with its delightful sing-song, and quaint dialect. I brooded over this trouble more and more, though it was not the only one which depressed me now. I fell ill with fever, and on my recovery the sad news arrived that my elder brother had died, and that my father would never recover from the shock of his death. I was entreated to return home immediately, but alas! I was too late!

*　　*　　*　　*　　*　　*

I will pass over the first days of my return. Ah! the dear old hall looked beautiful as ever, standing in the park, with the noble oaks and cedars. Yes! there was no outward change, but gone for ever were those who made the place so dear to me. And had I also lost the beloved Suffolk dialect? No, these were the words I heard on first going into the village :

" That hood dry, Jim ? "

" That that du, Tom bor ! "*

How delighted I was to hear these words! The dialect was not gone, but there was danger of its passing away. Now I must try to gather all I could of the old Suffolk sayings. By cottage fireside, or blacksmith's forge, at Hawkey supper, or shepherd's shed, or at the village shop I was always welcome; freely all would talk to Master Archie (as they still called me). They would say,

---

* Meaning, " It keeps dry, Jim ! "　" Yes it does, Tom, bor ! "

" Master Archie, we don't fare as how you'll put us in no book, so we don't mind a-telling of you all mander of what, we don't."

If you sit down with me under the fine old chestnut trees on the village green, I will tell you a little about the surrounding houses and cottages.

There, half hidden by trees, with a garden aglow with old-fashioned flowers, the vines nearly covering the white-washed walls, is the house of the wise woman of the village. Ninety years old or over is Old Mother Callow; no one remembers her to be young, and all are sure that she can work cures on young and old far better than any doctor in the land. If any one dare to doubt this, he would be looked upon as having " no know."

There, not far from her dwelling, is a low-roofed thatched cottage still called the Spinning School, where formerly a busy hum of wheels was heard, for on a summer afternoon through the open door you could see many girls intent on the important work of learning to spin. Round flew the buzzing wheels, each girl anxious to finish her hank of wool first, and try to spin the finest thread, and woe to the girl who in haste would twitch the thread so tightly as to break it, for down came a switch on her back from the old dame, Gammer Grey, who would call out,

" Now, mawther, take that.   I'll larn yow to be a toad."

Old Gammer was forced to be cross; she always had the "misery in her head along of all the wind they spinning wheels made." No one could tell how the wind managed to reach her head though, for it always had on it an immense black bonnet of the coal-scuttle shape, and inside a thick cap, whose frills of white net so hid her brown old face that you had to peer long and intently before it dawned upon you.

Ah, in the winter afternoons many were the trials, for rush-light was a mockery, and poor old Gammer would be "nigh out on her head," as threads would be broken so often, and when she tried to teach the girls to join the thread again with the weaver's knot, why how could she see? The knot would come undone, and the girl would burst out laughing, and be sure to be sent home after enjoying a good box on her ears. Of course, a scene of this kind was a joy to all her companions. But now the angry Gammer would look fiercely round, knocking her stick on the brick floor, and crying out,

"Spin, you lazy mawthers, dew. Tew candles a-burning an' not a wheel turning."

That's the village inn you see there, with a plot of grass before its porch, on which are feeding ducks and geese, the property of the landlord; and on the seats under the wooden porch are the villagers resting and busy talking over the important affairs of crops, weather, or in lower tones, perhaps, the news of Farmer Smith "a-going for to drop the wages come Saturday," etc.

There, not far from the inn is the blacksmith's forge, the familiar sound of the hammer, the bright light, with the sturdy figure of Tom Mann, the blacksmith, at his forge, making a perfect picture.

These cottages round this village green have each pleasant gardens, and many groups of children may always be seen and their merry voices heard singing in broad Suffolk dialect the old songs, as they play and dance over the green. The farmhouses scattered here and there are always alive with busy sounds of farm work, the lowing of cattle, and the cackling of hens and geese. And there stands the village shop, adorned outside with strings of onions, pumpkins, etc., and inside—pray be careful to stoop when you go in, or away will go your cap, for bunches of tallow candles hang from the low ceiling, in company with dangling boots, and other merchandise. Yonder to the right the ancient round tower of the old church is seen half hidden among the thick trees.

But the Rectory, standing far back in its grounds, is entirely hidden, as the rector never lets the trees be cut down or thinned. For Mr. Danvers believed that Nature should not be interfered with; however, he was only eccentric on this point, and was kind and gentle, and much beloved by all.

Had I time I could show you, in the grassy lanes, groups

of cottages which were in former years well known as the homes of the very poorest of Beechwood village, the cottages even now looking uncared for compared with the rest of the dwellings, as if they could not rise above the taint of former years, when they were the homes of redoubtable prize-fighters and smugglers far too well known in all the country side, whose hidden closets were often full of goods, in days gone by, ready to be sold by packmen or traders only too glad to help in turning them into money, and sure to keep the smugglers' secret well.

On my return to Beechwood, my old friend, the shepherd, Pleasance by name, was one of the first to greet me warmly. He was the great oracle of the village as to the weather. His cottage stood at the edge of the common, a perfect picture of rustic beauty. The low-thatched roof and white-washed clay walls were gay with roses and honeysuckle; the diamond-paned windows, picturesque as they were to the eye, certainly did not let in much light, but by the house-door was a wooden seat, where, on most summer evenings, old Master Pleasance was to be seen sitting smoking his beloved pipe, and there came the neighbours to hold grave consultations, especially when crops had to be gathered in, and very seldom was he wrong in his forecasts, though the old shepherd at times certainly made use of his imagination. For instance—the winter just passed had been icy cold, such frost as the oldest man never remembered, so, of course, Master Pleasance was consulted as to the reason by the villagers, who all accepted his explanation without any doubt, as they sat together one Saturday evening in the kitchen of the village inn, each man with his pipe in his mouth, and a brown mug of his beloved beer before him on the long table.

" Coold, masters," cried Pleasance; " why that should be stammen cold! Look you hare; the old sun ha' turned tew far to the north, he hev." But old Pleasance shall now speak for himself.

" Lork, Master Archie, that du fare like old times to see you along on us agin, that du. Yes, Master Archie, you're right, the old days was the best. Folks fare to have lost their ' know.' I count there's too many new books, an' they set an' read 'um, one on the top of another, till they get right ' dunt,' poor dears, they du. Why, when my father was a young man you could go an' get your fortune told as plain as a pike-staff for a matter of half-a-crown, you could. That was along of the stars they larnt that; but lork! now they don't take no trouble about they, Master Archie, none what-somever. Look you hare, Master Archie, my wife she lar right bad, an' my son was gone over the sea, and we han't heard nothin' of him for tew years an' nine days; well, my poor wife she *was* in a way, an' I was wholly stammed, an' what to do I din't know.

" Well, one day an old packman he come by, an' says he to me,

" ' Master,' you look right mawldy, you du.'

" So I up an' told him, an' he says,

" ' You jist go to Cambridge; there's a wonderful clever man there along of the stars, an' they pay him to set an' look at um.'

" So off I set, bein' as my Joe could look after the ship (sheep). Well, I walked all the way to Cambridge, an' right tired I was. I had to stop an' get a rest at the ' Ram an' Goat,' I can tell you; but, howsomdever, when I got there, they shew me where the wise man lived—that was a big house. They let me in, an' I set down in a room; the walls was all kivered up with book-shelves, an', lork, there, there was a sight o' books on 'um.

" Well, at last a little man cum in; he looked right kind, he did, I will say, an' he up an' asked me what I wanted. So I told him, an' asked him to draw out my fortune. I told him I was born under the planet Mars, an' I tell the year an' the month, an' my son's too, I did.

" Well, poor man, he looked that overseeun he din't fare to know what to say. But at last says he,

" ' My good man, I am very sorry, but I cannot do anything for you.'

" I con't speak for a mirrit when he said that, Master

Archie, that I con't.   But lork, I was that angry, an' at last
I up an' says, says I,

"'Look you hare, sir; what good ha' yew got out of all
yar high larning, an' set here an' draw all that power o'
money, as I hare you du, along of minding the stars, an'
then you sar as how you can't tell me nothing.   I consate
you 'ont tell me.'

" So I shew him half-a-crown, and says,

"'If you 'ont go an' tell me nothing more, is my boy comin'
home, or is he drownded?'

" Well, he looked that dottled, I con't make him out nohow.   I could see he was no good, so I flung out of the
room, an' home I cum."

The blacksmith's forge vied with the kitchen of the ale-
house in attracting the village folk, for here was news to be
gathered from the waggoner stopping to have his horses' feet
looked at, or the carriage on its way to the town.   My old
friend, the waggoner, Jim Scarf, greeted me with a broad
grin of pleasure the first evening I found him slowly approach-
ing the blacksmith's.   So much the same he looked, as I
ever remembered him, his dust-coloured smock, slouching
hat, and red handkerchief round his neck, the whip in his
hand, so little used, for Boxer and Smiler were like
brothers to him, and obeyed his " Whoa, come hither," or
" Whoa, come hather," without even a toss of the head, and

they looked at him with real affection in their eyes, while he tied the bag on their mouths, from which they ate their well-earned noon-day meal.

"Ah, yar! Master Archie," cried Jim; "I heard tell as you was on the road back home, an' lork, when we heard that, why, we all hollared for a pint of best, everyone on us, we did, bein' we was in the ale-house, an' in come the landlord, an' got the ale, an', says he,

"'Drink all of you, my lads, to Master Archie, an' I'll stand the beer, and may God bless him an' keep him along on us.'

"Well, I warrent we din't leave none of the beer behind, an' that loud we hollared nigh took the oud roof off, Master Archie. Well, now, that is kind on yer, Master Archie, an' I must not call you 'Sir Archibald.' Yes, Saturday I shall be at home, an' lork! there ain't none on us as 'll forget to come to the hall to supper—to your welcome home supper—an' we'll bring our old songs in our hids, Master Archie, I'll warrant yer!"

Never can I forget the Saturday when all my old friends came to the hall to supper. The old-fashioned kitchen, with the black oak beams crossing each other on the ceiling, the long table down the middle of the room, and cross tables by the windows, all full of well-remembered friends. Though Time had thrown snow over some heads, and bent some backs, formerly so erect, he could not change the friendly look in the faces, or alter their voices.

"Three cheers for Master Archie!" That sound will ring in my ears all my life. "Welcome home, Master Archie," and three cheers more greeted me. As I stood up at the head of the table to welcome my friends, how misty my eyes were, and as to my voice, not one word could I speak for ever so long; but my old servants were just as bad. And how glad I was when the clatter of knives and forks began, and the roast beef and mutton had to be devoured!

Well, the old songs were sung, and many of them are so well known to my readers that I need not give them here. But at last after very much persuasion the stolid John Darkens was goaded to stand up and sing, after drinking a long draught of beer. Clearing his throat many times, he began in a loud voice the words:

> " Larn tew be wise !
> Laarn tew be wise !
> Laaarn tew be wise ! "

Then again,

> " Laaaarn tew be wise ! "

and each time raising his voice to a higher Suffolk "squick."

At last came a great knocking on the table, all the men calling out,

"Lork, John, wa' can't you gon we no more nor that, bor?"

Upon which the singer looked all round, and calling out, "You larn that fust," sat down with stolid dignity.

A great laughter followed this song, though they had been accustomed every year to hear it from John at the Hawkey Supper.

"Now, come, gon us a song, Steggles, du. Lork! yar hid that is full o' songs."

Steggles, after much pressing, began,

"THE FARM THAT PAYS."

The Farmer goo to market,
   An' Johnny goo to plough,
The Missus mind the baby,
   An' Dolly milk the cow ;
An' Sally feed the piggies,
   An' the chickabidies too ;
An' the baby clap that's hands tew hare
   The cockadooledoo !

Chorus—

   The folks as goo, an' farm that way,
    Will olust have a farm that pay.

I cannot give all the speeches which followed, though they would form a complete lesson to my readers in the broad Suffolk dialect.

How rejoiced I was to hear the words of love and reverence

for my father's memory. Well they knew what he had done for Beechwood, making their lives happy and prosperous; and I determined to keep true to his noble purpose, and even start fresh plans for their prosperity.

It was Tom Mann, the blacksmith, who spoke of their love to my father, and what he had done for them.

"Yes," cried Tom, rapping the table as loud as if he thought it was his anvil. "Yes, masters, I used for to say, if all the landlords was to du as he du, why folks wouldn't du as they du du. Why, there was stacks fired, and barns burnt down, and all mander of things done, to spite some of the gret people." Then, contrasting my father with one whom all disliked, not without good reason, for he was proud, cruel, and hard to the people, and detested my father, who would often plead the cause of the poor with him: "And things would har been much worse, han't it been for Miss Winifred; why, folks ha' sin her cry and go down of her knees to try and get her father to be kinder to the people."

Now came a parting cheer, and many good wishes from all my old friends, ending with the old shepherd, who stood up and cried out,

"Masters, du you all jine in three cheers for the lady we hope'll be Master Archie's wife before long."

Ah, they did cheer heartily, more loudly than ever now.

I shook hands in reply with all my guests. They had discovered why I had been every day to Arlington Hall.

I cannot in this paper find space for introducing my readers to all my friends, rich and poor, but they must go with me to visit Mother Callow, tht wise woman of Beechwood. Here you shall have her first greetings in her own words, without any interruption from me, and you will learn the great secret of my life from her.

This was her greeting on my entering her cottage.

"Master Archie, bless your handsome face. I consated as you'd soon come an' see me. They foreign parts have made you as brown as a berry. I can't frame to say 'Sir Archibald;' 'Master Archie' you'll allways bee to me. Lork! how time du fly. I'm on my ninety, I am, come next Christmas Dar, January 6th. Ah, they wicked min to go an' alter Christmas Dar. Could our dear Lord be born twice? No, I never ate no plum-puddin' on December 25th. No, Master Archie, not if the Queen was to send some.

"They du say you are not going over the sea no more; ah, there's many a one is glad an' proud to hear that, an' I know one, live not far from here, as will fare more lightsum now. There, set down on the stool, Master Archie, where you used to set years ago, an' tell me all about the sweet young lady, an' no shame either, for I nursed your dear mother to the day she died, an' heard a deal o' the ins and outs of things. No, Miss Winifred has sin a deal since you went away; they wanted her to marry young Sir John, but no, she would never look at anyone. I tell you true, Master Archie, your dear mother gave me a likeness of you, an' she would sit an' look at it for long, long, she would. Sir George he was that angry because she wouldn't marry them that wanted her, so they sent her off to see a lot of places, but nothing changed her, so home she come, an' then Sir George, you know, died out hunting.

"Ah, Master Archie, when I heard as you was so ill in foreign parts, why I knew that was Sir George's unkind letters as had done it. Why, if he din't go an' sar you had wholly given up our young lady! But there, he's dead an' buried, poor man. They du say he walk, but I've never sin him, so that I must leave, an' I know you never say nothing to nobody about our young lady away or at home, foreby* if he du walk, he con't hare nothin'. But pray, don't you go acrost the old churchyard in the dark. If he walk anywhere that's in the churchyard. He's on ghosts' land there, an' they old ghosts, why they fare stronger there nor anywhere else; everybody know that much about them; so you see he'd catch a hode on you in a mirrit, an' du you a mischief.

---

* Suffolk for " because."

" He was right a malusful man, he was, an' lork, what would he frame to be now? Ah, I've sin a deal of old ghosts in my day, an' I warrent I know a deal along of their conivers an' conovers,* I du. You see, Master Archie, they fare to be kept down a deal more nor they used for to be in my mother's days, foreby there's such a lot of chapels built up now, an' they keep 'um down good tidy. But lork, when my mother was a gall, folks could see they ghosts a-walking about as bold as brass. She run home one evening acrost of a meddar, by Dead Man's Lane, that was, an' there she see an old ghost set up on the gate, a-swinging of his legs good tidy, that fared to snare at her, that did. She knew he wanted to ketch a hode on her when she come to climb over that gate, but she was tew sharp for him. There was a hole in the hedge, an' she got through that, an' when she come to look round, he was gone.

" My father says he cum home one night from the hall; he'd been a sheep-shearing, an' if he din't see two old ghosts a-walking, looking as bold as bold with hats on their hids, right of the middle o' the road! They never so much as framed to turn a mite out of the way for him; so bein' as my father was a wonful strong-headed man, an' never see no fare of nothin', he won't go an' turn out on his way for they,

* Suffolk for strange ways.

so if he din't go an' walk right through them, that he did. My mother she up an' asked him what they felt like.

"'Wonful like wool,' says he, 'but lork, my smock that smelt that strong of brimstone for weeks after,' says he, 'so I wished I had gone an' left 'um alone, I did.'

"But there, bless me, talking all about they old ghosts. Well, 'tis my head wanders.

"Miss Winifred she spend her time among the poor folks, an' see to the children, she du, an' all that. I never see her look so beautiful as she du now. Why, I set at church an' look at her, an' can't take my old eyes off. I knew as you was a-coming home along of my Star Book, Master Archie. That never tell me wrong. I keep that safe in my oud Mingen Hutch* along of The Wud,† an' I tell Miss Winifred as you was a-coming, and here you set!

"Well, both Sir George an' your father are gone now, and I fare sure all will come round as that should be; and, Master Archie, I am proud to think you've come to tell me first of all. Bless you both; an' that's the lovely di'mond ring you're going to give her? An' me not to guess you'd been up there the first thing! Ah, but the dear old hall will be like old days agin.

* Old cak chests where many different things were kept—in one division bread, etc., in another the beloved scarlet cloak, best bonnet, etc.
† Suffolk for the Bible.

Look, look! There she cum! driving they beautiful chestnut ponies. Bless you, both on you; and give her this blush rose to shame it, with her two cheeks!"

NOTE.—The Suffolk dialect is not given broadly, in pity for hose who do not understand it.

Young Sir Archibald showed his love for Suffolk in many ways more important than the subject of dialect. It grieved him much on his return home to see the population leaving the country for the town, and he determined to do what he could to prevent this. He saw in other counties how the growth of fruit, the rearing of fowls of all kinds, and greater thrift among the rural population, increased their general prosperity, and with zeal he now set to work to remedy if possible the evil he deplored.

Other landowners would shake their heads as they saw his plans of giving small holdings to some of the work-people at a low rent, and helping them to start their cultivation, etc. Also how he improved and widened the river to make a water way to carry Beechwood produce to markets far and near.

But I have not space here to explain all he did for the prosperity of the village. He well knew that the secret of keeping the population in the country was to make it possible for them to find work and food without seeking it elsewhere.

"Come to Beechwood," he said to those who opposed him, for well he knew that statistics are uninteresting, arguments are not convincing, advice is aggravating. Consult surer evidence, and find it in the apple-faces of school children, arrayed like the flowers of the field, and seated in shining rows in some country church, singing with joyful voices, and hardly-suppressed smiles,

"I am horribly afraid, because of the ungodly that forsake Thy law."

These children are growing up among pasture-lands and country gardens. They feast on real bread, and milk from the cow; their "dumplin's and tracle" and apple "hoglins" have not been preserved in tins. Their parents have the meadow instead of the midden outside the door. There is a "beautiful drying ground," where the week's "wash" flaps in an untainted breeze, and the rose looking in at the window has power to banish rags and "oddments," so that the eye is trained to recognise Heaven's first law of order, and this law will bring a blessing on the land that it may be fruitful and multiply; and while England remains, seed-time and harvest shall not cease.

> Call Suffolk "Silly?"
>   'Twould be worse than murder;
> Has she not given us
>   Our noble "Sirdar?"

HOW OUD POLLY GORST "CUM AGIN."

Scene in the Widder's House, Banningham.

A N óld-fashioned low-roofed room, open chimney, with fire on the hearth, seats along the chimney corners, on which sit Widder Andrews, Widder Beales, Widder Stimpson, Bet Scarf, and Billy Gorst (otherwise Silly Billy). The widders seem in great trouble, groaning loudly and rocking backwards and forwards, Billy smoking a short pipe, and kicking the cat whenever the widders are not looking. Through the diamond-paned window they now see a young lady coming up the path to the cottage. Billy puts his pipe into his pocket and escapes by the back door.

Miss Mary from the hall enters. All the widders get up and make their "obedience," but do not leave off groaning, except to say,

"Bless you, dear Miss Mary, for a-coming to see we poor widders. That fare a sight of months as you ha' bin awar, that du, and we ha' missed you good tidy! O lorks, O lorks, for to think what we ha' come tew. But now we shall ha' someone for tew dole tew, we shall, Miss Mary."

" Yes, yes, do tell me all about your troubles, pray! I am so sorry to see you all so miserable."

" Ah! we du concate as you are our friend, Miss Mary, soo we'll tell you all about that fust and last, we widders will. Look you hare, Miss Mary, you know this hare house was guv to Banningham only for widders, that was. Well, if the 'Budd'* din't goo an' put in oud Polly Gorst an' her son, Silly Billy. We widders hollared out good tidy, when they come, we did. Why, miss, I du sar that was breaking of the law about the widders' house. We was to live here in peace, an' squat without no min to trouble, and we are too oud to stand Billy's noise. Mrs. Anders an' me is on our ninety-four, an' Mrs. Stimpson is on her ninety-eight, an' Bet Scarf is on her eighty-seven. Well, I sar we widders fared right comfortable as we poor widders can ever hope to be afore Polly Gorst come in here. But, lork! we never had a squat day since she cum, the oud toad! But, lork, miss, we han't no mander o' quiet after she cum; we con't do nothin' to please her, and she was a-scoldin' all dar and a-cryin' all night. Yes, miss, she were the most horrid, miserable oud toad; and as to Billy, why he stolt our things, an' sold 'um

---

* Budd, the name for Parish Overseers.

fur to buy backy with, an' she got wus and wus, she did. But one dar she was took ill, an' she died. Lork, miss, how pleased we widders was.

"But, s'ars o' mine, if she din't 'Come agin.' The fust time she cum were like this. Mrs. Bales an' I we lar up of the chamber, an' poor Mrs. Stimpson she lar downstairs in the room, foreby she brook her leg, last bane settin' as ever was, poor dare. Miss Mary, she was a-climbin' up of the ladder to goo on the chamber, an' lork! if she din't go an' topple backwards-way down. She han't her sights on, she han't, an' there is two rungs out on the ladder, an' she din't know it. Well, she lar a-dollerin' on the bricks all on a hape. We widders we con't hope her up nohow, but we see oud Quack Darkins a-gooin' by, an we got him to hope her up on the bed, an' there she lar a matter of six weeks, she did, afore she cum tew. Soo, miss, as I was a-sayin', Mrs. Bales an' me an' Bet lar on the chamber there tew beds there.

"Well, just as Mrs. Anders was a-gooin' to sleep, she fared to hare a noise, an', lork, if she din't see oud Polly Gorst as plain as plain cum shufflin' into the room. She must ha' cum through the key-hole; that there door was shut an' the window tew. Up she cum to the bed of the side she used to lar on, an' she hove an' hove at the pillar to make that comfortable, an' then she got into the bed, an' there she lar, she did, till the morren. Well, Mrs. Anders she

never spoke to her; she just turned round an' went off to
sleep, an' when she woke in the morren, why, oud Polly was
gone!

" ' Why, she felt like a bundle of fluff,' said Mrs. Anders.

" And arter that dar we widders we han't no squat why the
oud toad! She won't wait like a dacent ghost till that was
dark; she cum a shufflin' an' a frimicken' about all dar. You
see, miss, if she got a shillin' guv her, why she goo an' hide
that under the bricks, soo we concate she cum for to look
for 'um. Yes, miss, I warrant we was wholly done.

" Lork, miss, why Bet Scarfe she was a-cummin' home
round by the pond the other dar, an' if she didn't see oud
Polly sit on the top of the gate as bold as brass. How she
did snare at Bet, an' she tried to kitch a hold on her, but
Bet she picked up a horse-shoe, lar on the road, an' she
copped that at oud Polly, an' if she din't see that oud horse-
shoe go right through her, that did. Bet she run awar, an'
when she looked back, why, Polly was gone.

" There, Miss Mary, I mam't goo on all dar, only what
I sar is we han't no mander of squat night nor dar.
Folks goo an sar as how that all cum of the rats, drottle 'um!
Why, miss, they don't know nothin' belong to oud ghosts,
they don't. Dear Miss Mary, you know better, an' that due
us good to dole about it. Ah, good-bye, miss, an' thank you
for your kind present. We'll get some comfort with it."

A day or two after Miss Mary called again on the widders.

"Ah, Miss Mary, bless you for cummin' agin, an' we've good news to tell you. After you went away last time we set a dollerin', foreby that oud ghost she cum wus than ever a-scuppin' at the bricks like mad, an' looking in at the winder an' laughin' at us. When we wus at the wus the door ope'd, an' who should cum in but Mrs. Caller, the wise woman.

"'Well,' says she, 'you du look miserable, you du. I set last night a-connin' of my Star Book, an' I fared to hare a voice sar, "goo an' see them oud widders," so I've cum to hare what's the matter.'

"Well, we tode her all about Polly fust an' last. She never spok a wud, but she sat for half an hour a-thinkin'. At last she hollared out, 'I'll settle her,' and awar she went. Well, the next dar she cum agin, an' she set down a-laughin' fit to bust. 'Lork! I ha' wholly done her,' says she, when she could spake.

"Look you here. I ha' been in an' out among ghosts all my life, an' I know a deal about 'um. I allust keep a lot o' branches of the aspin tree under my bed to keep the Evil One off. Our dear Lord's cross wus made of that wood, an' soo the leaves are allust all of a tremble. That wood that's the strongest charm you can get. Well, I took a bundle of them branches along of me, an' off I went to yer churchyard, jest afore the ould sun wus agoin' to get up, an' if I din't see oud Polly a-creepin' into her grave, safe an' sure. Well, I set to work an' I bound they branches acrost an' acrost of her grave, I did. I fared to hear a sort of a wimperin' when I'd done, but I says, ' You ha' got to lar where you are now !'

" Well, Miss Mary, we din't here nothin' last night, an' we fare right happy agin. How we thank Mother Caller; and we all had a comforable cup of tea together."

Miss Mary congratulated the widders, but did not tell them her father had sent the rat-catchers, who had killed a sturdy family of rats in their back-yard, nor did she tell them of a visit she had paid to the gamekeeper's wife, who was a relation of Polly Gorst, an' whom she found in a great rage at the report of Polly's "walking." She did tell them, though, that her father had sent Billy Gorst to the workhouse.

" Why, look you here, Miss Mary," she cried, " if she got to the good place she won't want to cum back."

" An' if she got to the bad place she won't ha' the chance ! "

A WISE WOMAN OF THE OLDEN TIME STILL·LIVING IN A SUFFOLK VILLAGE (1892).

(Scene in a lonely cottage—Old woman and grand-daughter living there—Extracts from conversations held with the Wise Woman of the village and the Squire's daughter — Young lady at door.)

LORK, now! if I din't frame to think that was my hin a-scrapin'! Du come in, Miss Rosy. Bless yar pretty face! an' how is the lady at the hall? Ah, thank her, du, for that bufful bit o' beef; how I should like that to-morror for my dinner!

"Sall, come you forrud an' bring a plate tew lar that on. An' mind you kiver that up; 'don't the cat'll ha' it, sure enough.

"Du come, Miss Rosy, an' set close to me. I'm on my eighty-eight, an' I don't fare tew hare as well as I did. You see, miss, I ha' the misery in my owd hid that bad that I scurse know nothin' at times. How I cum to kotch that soo bad was when I went to the spinning school. You see, miss, there wus a sight o' wheels alust a-twirling and a-turning about, an' that made sich a wind. My hid worn't as strong as them other morthers as went there. You see, my father he fell off a waggon onter his head, an' lorks! they thought he was dead; but he cum tew, he did. But that's nathere here nor there. Now what was that you asked me about, miss? Ah! them ghostesses, that was it. Poor things! Why, I've bin in an' out o' them all my life. I don't reckon much of they ghostesses. Why, they can't nather brew nor bake; but lork! there's no end to their frimmucks and kenivers,* I can tell you. You never know what they'll be up tew next.

" Well, miss, as I was a-going to say, my darter Bet she was a wonful masterful sort of a gal, an' she must gooo an' marry that Jim Sims. He never was no good, and he turned out as bad as bad could be; an' lork! if he 'din't go an' drink hisself to dead in a year an' a day!

" Soo she cum back to me, she an' her baby, and she lar in the room next to mine. Well, one night she cum to my bedside all of a flutter an' a dither, an' I says I,

" ' Gal, what's the matter? '

* For queer ways and tantrums (old Suffolk).

"'Matter!' says she, 'o lork! if I din't hare Jim as plain as plain could be a-callin' out, "Bet! Bet! Bet!" I was that skared, but I din't sar nothin'.'

"I says I, 'Gal, gooo you an' lar down agin; an' if that hollar out agin you must up an' arnser that, an' sar, "What du you want?"'

"Well, sure enough, as soon as she lar ·down of her bed again she hard that call out louder, 'Bet! Bet! Bet!' so she up and said, 'What du you want?' an' that said, as plain as plain could be,

"'Gooo you to the old shod; mind you gooo right alone, an' gooo when the old moon is up; don't you take no light along of you. You must take my pick, an' gooo to the left side o' the shod, an' then you count thirteen bricks in the wall from the arth, an' take the pick an' pull out that brick you'll find a puss o' gowd.'

"Well, Bet she kum an' towd me, and I says I,

"'Gall, you gooo an' du jest as he towd you. Don't you want find nothin'.'

"But lork a sarsay! My Bet she was that masterful she con't gooo that night, howsumdever, for that was morning then. But the next night if she din't gooo an' get that morther, Kitty Flanam, to gooo along of her! She feared skerred to gooo all alone.

"Well, they went to the owd shod, an' she counted her

bricks, an' when she cum to thirteen, she up an' took the pick, and she huled out the brick fast enough. But lork! when that brick cum out, if there was nothin' behind that but a few rusty owl nails!

" All the time they was a-doin' of this they heard horrid noises, and smelt a dreful smell o' sulpher. When Bet cum back an' told me all this, I says I,

" ' Gall, look you hare, you should ha' done just as that towl you, an' you'd had your puss o' gowd in your hand now. Now, I warrant we shall have no manner o' rest night or day for that varmint of a ghost.'

" Well, I never spok' a trewer wud! If that din't come a-roarin' and a-rampin' round the hous' night an' day, an' a-callin' of Bet down the chimley, till I con't stan' that nooo longer. Sooo I says I,

" ' Lork a sarsay me! Bet, gooo you an' arst the parson to cum an' lar this owl ghost. An', gall, look you hare, tell him too be sure to goo an' bring the Wud* along of him; don't he con't du nothin'! '

" Well, he cum, an' he kinder held back. Poor dear old gentleman, he was a wunful *quit* man; he won't hut a fly. But lork! I du believe he din't know a pig from a ship, though he was mighty high-larned. Well, I towd him I was right ill, along of being kep' awake by a nastur oud ghost,

---

* Bible in Suffolk dialect.

an' I prayed him to lar that. Well, miss, I du hope he was not a-laughen, but he looked out o' the winder kinder 'per-meritatin' like, till I fared right angry, an' I up an' says,

"'Sir, what use is all that high larnin' as you got off of college, if you can't even lar a poor ghost?' says I. Sooo when it kum tew I had tew tell him what to du.

"'Why, sir,' says I, 'you have for tew say the Lord's Prayer backards-way, with the "Wud" under yar arm.'

"Well, he said the prayer to hisself; but lork! I con't hare if he did it right arter all !

"'Now, sir,' says I, 'you must cum along of me.' Sooo out we went, an' says I, 'Now, sir, you hare that oud ghost a-howlin' an' a-roaring about the house. Well, you have just to call out as loud as ever you can, "How woll yar be laid?"'

"Well, the roaring an' the howlin' went on wus when I sar this. But he did call out good tidy loud,

"'How woll yar be laid?'

"But, drottel him, if he din't sar he din't hare nothin'! Howsumdever, he wus as deaf as a stone; don't he would ha' heard the oud ghost hollar out,

"'I'll be laid by fire an' water.'

"'Bet,' says I, 'goo you in an' bring a rush-light candle, an' the tinder box and matches.'

"'Now, sir,' says I, 'du you see this hare ditch?'

"'Yes,' says he; 'I du.'

" ' Well, now, sir, that ghost say that'll be laid by fire an' water. Soo look you hare; this is the manner of it. You must take the candle in yar hand lighted, and you must jump right over that there ditch. But mind you jump quick, or the oud ghost that'll ketch a houd of you! Well, as you jump you must throw that candle inter the water. You must kop it right behind you, an' as that snaste (wick) of that candle gooo out, why that ghost that'll be laid safe an' sure! But lork! mind you jump quick, an' keep the blessed Wud tight under yar arm! '

" Well, the poor old gentleman war right feared of jumpin'. (That were a wide ditch, that were.) But at last he ketched a howd o' the candle an' he lep' over. But lork! if he din't throw that candle afore him instud of behind, an' he din't jump half quick enough, so the owd ghost caught a howd of him—that caught a hode of his arm; an' then, lork! how that roared round; but as soon as that candle was in the water, that hissed like an oud sarpent, an' that went out all of a blue flame, an' such a smell o' sulpher there wus. The poor old gentleman was wholly done; howsomdever, we con t help that.

" Bet and I we went round by the gate, an' when we come to him, there he lar in a swand. Bet an' I we kinder carried him inter the cottage, and guv him a little gin, an' arter an hour or so he cum tew. But his poor arm—that was all scrunched up of his side, an' that never cum right, never no more tew his dyin' day; an' when he lar of his coffin, that was scrunched up just the same.

"You see, miss, he din't du what I toud him. If he had kopt that candle behind him as he lep', you see, the oud ghost that *must* ha' been 'laid' when the candle went out in the water, but foreby he kept that before him the oud ghost that passed him, an' ketched houd of him.

"Howsumdever, my Bet an' I we never heard no more of the oud ghost—that were 'laid,' sure enough; but my Bet she went off an' tuk a place, an' then if she din't goo and marry the tea-man; he cum round every month a-sellin' tea! Drettle the man! we din't want no tea in them days, a-wasting money on such stuf. But there, I got to like that right enough before long.

"Well, the tea-man he had a cart, an' he druv about the country from week end tew week end, an' his wife were dead, and he asked Bet to marry him; but he wunt have the child, sooo I kep' that.

"Well, miss, that gal du mind me o' what I was at her age. My mother she was what they call 'a wise woman,' an' she taught me a deal, she did. Folks cum to her for to be cured o' all mander o' what, an' she never so much as took a penny off of anyone. An' she never would let they gooo for to thank her when they got well. She towd them that was all done by 'one up a-top,' soo accordingly they must thank Him, an' pray to Him as she did when they cum to her. An' bein' as you ha' bin sooo kind to me, Miss Rosy, I'll larn you a few o' the things she taught me. (Only you can't du nothin' till I'm dead an' buried.) Then sooo be.

"If anyone cum to you for to be cured of a burn, you must take a hode of the part that's burnt, an' th'en draw the forefinger of your right hand round the burn three times three, you must. An' you must sar to yourself as you du this:

> "'There cum two angels out o' the East,
>   One brought fire, an' one brought frost,
>   Out fire! in frost!
>   In the name of all the heavenly host.'

"They must cum three times to you, an' you du the same; but you marnt tell um what you sar, an' they marnt thank you, don't that 'ont du they a mite o' good.

"If any folks cum to you with a thorn or a splinter o' wood in um, you must ketch a hode of the part where the wood is, an' you must say to yourself (after you've drawn your finger round the place three times three times),

> "'The Saviour Christ was born,
>   Crucified by a thorn,
>   The thorn was blessed,
>   An' so was He,
>   Never more to trouble thee.'

" You must du this four days runnin', and that will be sure
to be cured, that will; only they marnt pay you nothin'.

" There cum a poor man to me once, in a wonful low key
he were. He'd got a splinter in his hand, right by his thumb.
That were his right hand an' all! Well, he went to three
doctors, an' none of um count du nothin'; they say to him,
' If we cut inter yar hand, you'll ha' lock-jaw.'

" That was harvest-time, an' the poor man he had fifteen
children, an' he arnt eight shilling a week; an' lork! how
his poor wife cried; she cum along of him to me. Well, I
tuk to doctorin' of him my way; an' the swellin' that went
down, an' his hand that got right well, an' he tuk his harvest
an' never worked better in his life. Ah, lork, miss, you
never would believe the sight o' folks I ha' cured, some o'
one thing an' some of another. But, O dear, I wus strong
then, an' now I fare that wake I'm all of a dither an' a quither,
an' my breath that cum sooo hard, an' that is that short, I
don't fare to feel as if I han't no inside at all to spake of.
An' I'm sure I du my best fur to keep myself tewgether.
Why, miss, I take a good dose o' salts every mornin' as soon
as I git up, right on the top o' my heart! But I marnt talk
no more now, Miss Rosy; you cum agin soon, du, an' I'll
larn you how to cure the agar, an' the jaundice, an' a sight
o' other things. O dear a me! how my breath that du ketch
up. What a thing that is tew grow oud!

E

" But lork! I marnt talk o' bein' oud. There's old Jack Debvin on his ninety-five, an' he can crack a nut as well as anyone, an' ate that tew; and there's old Susan Cropin, if she ain't ninety-eight. They du say as she never had no sweetheart; she's as kedge as a rat, an' as cross as tew sticks, too!

" Well, good-bye, miss. I see that handsum Mr. Danford gone a-riding by just now; I warr'nt he gone tew the hall, an' I mustn't keep you, miss.

" Ah! bless you, miss, and thank you; that is kind! I shall get a little comfort for my rheumatism. I can't git up tew make my obedience, miss; don't I would, Miss Rosy, you know. Good-bye, miss."

L. A. FISON.

SOME SUFFOLK RIDDLES, SAYINGS, Etc.

MY Lord he went to London,
  My Lady went to Lynn,
My Lord he brought my Lady,
  A very pretty thing ;
Between two silver dishes,
  In four and twenty hours,
My Lord he brought my Lady,
  The fruit of all the flowers.

(Honey.)

Also another ending

My Lord he brought my Lady,
  A very pretty thing,
A well full of water—
  A garden full of flowers,
Can you tell my riddle
  In four-and-twenty-hours?

The King of Gibralta'
Built a great ship,
* An in the four corners
His daughter did sit.
If I tell you her name
I shall be much to blame !
For her name, that set in my riddle.

(*Ann*).

Black within,
Red without,
Four corners,
Like a clout.

(*A Chimney.*)

Little Miss Minafore
Wear a white pinafore,
The longer she sit
The shorter she grew.

(*A Candle.*)

Also

Little Miss Mew,
Sat in a pew !
The longer she sat
The shorter she grew.

(*A Candle.*)

Red Boy, make Black Boy's inside wobble.

(*Fire and Kettle.*)

* In Suffolk dialect " an " is used for " and."

Down in the medder

There sit Pat !

In a red petticoat

An a black hat.

(*Hips and Haws.*)

Up the street, down the street,

In at the winder,

An you never see nothin'.

(*The Wind.*)

There is a thing grow on a bed,

First 'tis green, and then 'tis red ;

There's not a lady in the land,

But what would take it in her hand

An put it in a hole before,

And wish she had ten thousand more.

(*Strawberry.*)

How many sticks go to the building of a crow's nest ? None ! for they are all carried to it.

In a garden was laid,

The most beautiful maid,

That ever appeared on a morn,

She became a man's wife

The first day of her life,

And died before she was born.

(*Eve.*)

What are the most unfriendly things in the world?　*Mile-stones*, for you never see two together.

What comes after* cheese?　(*Mice.*)

A shop full of meat, an no door to go in?　(*Nuts.*)

Why is a bad nut called deaf?　Because it don't hear the maggot a-hollarin' that's inside.

> I had a little sister,
> 　Went pip-a-peep,
> She walked in the rivers
> 　Though ever so deep ;
> She walked on the land,
> 　Though ever so dry,
> Now tell me this riddle,
> 　An tell me no lie.
> 　　　　(*The Moon.*)

What goes up when rain comes down?　(*Umbrellas.*)

Father, mother, sister, brother, run all dar, never catch one another?　(*Millsails.*)

> A Riddle, a riddle
> 　As I suppose,
> A hundred eyes
> 　And never a nose !
> 　　　　(*A Sieve.*)

* " After " in Suffolk is used for " for."

As round as an apple,

As deep as a cup,

All the king's horses

Can't pull it up.

(*A Well.*)

As round as an apple,

As big as a ball,

Reach from here

To London Town Wall.

(*The Sun.*)

What is that which goes from London to York without moving? (*The Road.*)

Round and sound,

Jist a pound,

And that only weigh an ounce.

(*Sovereign.*)

Forty crows sat on a tree,

A farmer shot one,

How many would be left?

None. Because all the others would fly away.

The beginning of Eternity,

The end of time and space,

The beginning of every end,

And the end of every place.

(*The letter E.*)

If you find a clover of two,
  Fold and wish ;
And put in your shoe,
  Home when you run.
If you find that's open,
  You'll have your wish,
For that's a token.

(It is lucky to find a clover leaf with only two instead of three parts.)

First part of song when there was danger of the French invasion.

The French are a-coming
  O dear, dear, dear !
A parcel of old women,
  Go sneer, sneer, sneer !
The French are a-coming
  O lork, lork, lork,
A parcel of old women,
  Go talk, talk, talk, etc., etc.

If Martinmas day
Howd fine an clear,
The shepherd as lief
See his wife on her bier.

If the oak's before the ash,
Have a summer full of splash.
If the ash before the oak,
Have a summer full o' choke.

" Whatever is to be, Wuzy ? "

Can any one fathom the meaning of this saying in Suffolk ?

> Good weight and measure
> Is heavenly treasure.

> Youth an summer
> Have no fuller.

And what does " fuller " mean ? we said to the old Suffolk man who had just spoken these words.

" Mane, Masters ? " said the old man, " mane ! Why that mane, ' they have noo follar,' that's what they mane, I says."

———

GLEANING TIME IN SUFFOLK.

(The song appeared in *Punch* forty years ago.)

> LISTEN yow—be quiet, bor !
>   The bell is tolling eight,
> Why don't you mind what you're about ?
>   We're allus kind of late.

> Now, Mary, get that mawther dressed,
>   Oh dear, how slow you fare,
> There come a lot o' gleaners now,
>   Maw, don't stand gawkin' there !

Now, Jane, goo git yow that 'ere coach,
 And put them pillers in ;
Oh ! won't I give it you, my dear,
 If I do once begin ?

Get that 'ere bottle too—
 Don't stand there and sneer,
What'll yar father say d'ye think,
 If we don't take his beer ?

Come Willie, Jane, where is he gone ?
 Goo yow and fetch that child,
If yow don't move them legs o' yourn,
 Yow'll ma'ak me kind o' riled.

There, lock the door, and lay the key
 Behind that 'ere old plate ;
An', Jimmy, you run on afore
 An' ope the whatefield gate.

Well, here we be at last—oh dare,
 How fast my heart du bate.
Now, Jane, set yow by this 'ere coach,
 And don't you lave your sate,

Till that 'ere precious child's asleep.
 Then bring yow that 're sack,
And see if you can't try to-day
 An' kinder bend your back.

You'll all wish when the winter comes,
    And yow baint got no bread,
That, for all brawlin' about
    Yow'd harder wrought instead.

For all yar farther's arn must go
    Old Skimmin's rint to pay,
An' Mister Last, the shoemaker,
    So work yow hard, I say.

Dear me ! There go the bell agin,
    'Tis seven, I declare,
And we don't 'pear to ha' got none,
    We ought to get our share.

The gleanin' don't fare to be worth nothin',
    But I think, as far as I can tell,
We'll try, somehow, a coomb to scratch,
    If we be 'live and well.

Collected by LOIS A. FISON.

THE OLD CUSTOM OF GIVING "EVERLASTING FLOWERS" TO A BRIDE.

A VERY pretty custom at one time prevailed in some parts of Suffolk when a young girl was betrothed. Some married friend would give her a small bunch of the yellow and white immortelle, called "everlasting love," and tell her to give it to her betrothed husband, and he would keep her love as long as he kept the immortelle.

Some twenty-seven years ago, a lady gave my mother a piece on her betrothal, and on her silver wedding day her husband showed her the same bunch of immortelle as fresh-looking as ever. The same lady, now grown old, gave me a sprig on the occasion of my betrothal, and this has been carefully preserved ever since by my husband. I asked if this custom had any origin, and the answer I received I have woven into a story.

Mrs. Osmond.
From a Suffolk Village Friend.

SPECIMENS OF SUFFOLK HUMOUR.

ONE evening a noise was heard in the back kitchen of a Suffolk country house. The master of the house went to see the cause, when, to his astonishment, he saw a man with a lantern in his hand coming in.

"Whatever do you mean by coming into my house?" cried the master of the house, going on to pour forth a flood of reproaches in language not mild by any means.

At last the intruder called out, "Ha' yau done?"

"Yes, I have," was the answer. "But I ask again—what are you come here for?"

"Courtin' yar cook," cried the man.

"Courting my cook!" roared the master. "Well, but what have you got a lantern for? When I went courting I never took a lantern."

The intruder slowly spoke with a broad grin. "Noo, I don't wonder at you not takin' noo lantern along of you. I ha' sin yar missus!"

Wizards in Suffolk.

It may seem strange at this day, but it is a fact that the
belief in wizards has not died out of Suffolk; for not
so many years since a Roman Catholic priest came to live
in a town in Central Suffolk. To his astonishment, no one
would take him in as a lodger. "No! he is a wizard," all
said, till at last he found one householder who opened her
doors to him. But she was strongly remonstrated with by
friends on this dangerous step!

The Tinder Box.

No box of matches were used in the old Suffolk days.
On the high mantelpiece over the kitchen fireplace you
would have seen the tinder box, in which was a flint and
a bar of steel; at the bottom you would see the tinder-black
burnt paper.

Well do I remember as a little girl being filled with wonder
on waking from sleep to see Cook sitting up in her bed, and
making sparks fly into a little box she had before her. She
had a stone in her hand and something she kept knocking it
with, which made the sparks fly out. Then I saw her take
a piece of stick in her hand, and after blowing into the box
for a minute she dipped the stick in; and she told me after
the stick had brimstone on it. And then a beautiful light

appeared, with which she lighted the rush-light in a tin candlestick which stood on the chair by her bed.

" O, Cook," I cried, " do let me make some pretty sparks."

" No, no," cried both the servants; " you go to sleep, missy, don't we shall tell nus about you. Why, that's only five o'clock, soo goo to sleep or you'll never have the treat of sleeping here again, as you begged and prayed for yesterday. You marn't never meddle with the tinder box, my dear. Don't you know

> " ' If little gals goo and play with the tinder,
> Why they fly all on fire and be burnt to a cinder.' "

This frightened me very much, and covering myself with my bed-clothes, I was soon fast asleep; but always looked with great longing when I saw the tinder box on the high kitchen mantelpiece.

From the Diary of an old Suffolk Lady.

Jarrold and Sons, Printers, Norwich, Yarmouth, and London.

Selections from Jarrolds' New Books.

NEW 5/- BOOK BY MISS M. M. BLAKE.

Crown 8vo, Cloth Gilt.

The Blues and the Brigands. By M. M. BLAKE

Author of "*The Siege of Norwich Castle*," "*When the Century was Young*," &c. Illustrated by R. THACKERAY BEDINGFIELD.

The author of "When the Century was Young," has, in her new book, "The Blues and the Brigands," once again laid her scene in France, choosing, this time, the period of the great revolution of 1789, and the following years. Many of the most stirring events of that memorable time are presented us in a series of vivid pictures—historically true and graphically related—linked together in a touching and simple love-story.

The illustrations are by Mr. R. Thackeray Bedingfield.

NEW AND POPULAR BOOK ABOUT BEARS.

Crown 8vo, Cloth elegant, 3/6.

Adventures of a Siberian Cub.

TRANSLATED FROM THE RUSSIAN BY LEON GOLSCHMANN. With Twenty-four Beautiful illustrations by WINIFRED AUSTEN.

This book, in which the strange adventures of a Siberian Cub are related, was originally written in Russian, and has already been translated into French, German, and Norwegian, proving equally acceptable in each of these several languages. For the English version, Mr. Leon Golschmann is responsible, and the work of illustration has been intrusted to Miss Winifred Austen, whose illustrations of "To Central Africa on an Iceberg" attracted so much favourable notice.

London: Jarrold and Sons, 10 and 11, Warwick Lane, E.C.

Of all Booksellers and at the Bookstalls.

MRS. MARSHALL'S NEW 5/- BOOK.

Crown 8vo, Cloth elegant, Illustrated.

By the North Sea:

OR, THE PROTECTOR'S GRAND-DAUGHTER. By MRS. EMMA MARSHALL, Author of "*In the East Country*," &c., &c. Illustrated by W. MILLER-SMITH. Fifth Thousand.

"Mrs Marshall's new story is good enough to be singled out from the common mass of Christmas literature. The interest centres in Mistress Bridget Bendysh, the grand-daughter of the Lord Protector Oliver Cromwell, whom she is said to have resembled more closely than any of his children or of his other grandchildren. Her portrait shows her to have been a woman of stately appearance and dignified manners, the type of the Puritan gentlewoman of her time. Mrs. Marshall has taken care to interweave her historical facts so as not to overbear the main narrative that holds them all together."—*Daily Chronicle.*

"A capital historical novel."—*Daily Telegraph.*

"The story is a beautiful one altogether from beginning to end, and the reader becomes intensely interested in the fortunes of sweet Albinia Ellis. It will rank among the most acceptable of books." — *Devon and Exeter Gazette.*

"This novel is really a contribution to Cromwellian literature. As such it possesses a special importance besides its strong interest otherwise, and so should be widely read."—*Leicester Chronicle.*

"A story of exceptional merit and interest to young folks as well as to a wider range of readers. It is full of lively incident. Its tone is healthy in every sense, and it will prove a very acceptable gift book to many, though young girls in particular will appreciate its instructive portraitures of a by-past age."—*Scotsman.*

"Mrs. Marshall interweaves her historical facts and her narrative very delightfully, and her production is an admirable volume for big girls. The story is brought out very prettily."—*Preston Guardian.*

"Mrs. Marshall's skill as a storyteller is well sustained in this most interesting book."—*Liverpool Courier.*

"It is a good book and worthy the reputation of the authoress."—*Manchester Courier.*

"Mrs. Emma Marshall's historical tales are too well known to need characterization here. This latest story from her pen is a pleasant picture of English life in the days of William and Mary. It is a sweet and wholesome book, and is well illustrated."—*Nottingham Express.*

"Mrs. Marshall's story is altogether a most entertaining one, well written and true to life.'—*Weekly Sun.*

London: Jarrold and Sons, 10 and 11, Warwick Lane, E.C.

Of all Booksellers and at the Bookstalls.

Selections from Jarrolds' New Books.

Selections from Jarrolds' New Books.

THE "FLEUR DE LYS" SERIES OF 5/- HISTORICAL NOVELS.

Crown 8vo, Cloth elegant, Illustrated.

Cuthbert, Lord of Lowedale,

By R. D. CHETWODE, Author of *"The Marble City," "The Fortune of the Quittentuns."* Illustrated by G. GRENVILLE MANTON. 2nd Edition.

This book tells the adventures of an English boy in France during the reign of Charles the Ninth. The hero forms one of the retinue of a French nobleman, and, while so serving, succeeds, with the assistance of a faithful friend, in baffling a treacherous plot, in rescuing his master, and in effecting the escape of a beleagured garrison. The narrative is written in the form of an autobiography, and gives an interesting and realistic picture of life and character in the Sixteenth Century.

"Mr. Chetwode has portrayed a stirring period in a stirring manner. Boys will appreciate his achievement."—*Daily Chronicle.*

"Mr. Chetwode's story is a good example of an historical romance, well and soberly told, and is cleverly illustrated."—*Saturday Review.*

"Bristles with wonderful adventures and hair-breadth escapes of the wildest improbability, while its love scenes as befits a book written only for healthy-minded boys, are as meagre as it is possible for them to be, and quickly lose themselves in a mist of illusion."—*Pall Mall Gazette.*

"A thrilling story of intrigue and adventure. It is not too much to say that there is not a dull page in the book. The plot is well laid, and the telling of the story is achieved in robust English . . . will have more than a passing influence on every boy reader who cherishes romance and heroism."—*Court Journal.*

"A dashing romance of the sixteenth century. The interest is partly English, partly French; the famous Valois princes, the Dukes of Anjou and Alencon, play parts in the interesting and varied drama."—*World.*

"Essentially a book of adventure, and will be read with unflagging interest by every boy who has the good fortune to get the chance of perusing it. The tone is thoroughly healthy, and one is interested in the 'Lord of Lowedale' from his first appearance to the time when he eventually 'comes to his own again.'"—*Devon and Exeter Gazette.*

"The story is a thoroughly entertaining one, and will more than repay perusal. Mr. Chetwode writes exceedingly well."—*Leicester Chronicle.*

"It is a powerfully-written tale, which may be commended to all readers, and should be peculiarly acceptable to boys."—*Lincoln and Stamford Mercury.*

London: Jarrold & Sons, 10 and 11, Warwick Lane, E.C.

Of all Booksellers and at the Bookstalls.

Selections from Jarrolds' New Books.

NEW BOOKS FOR BOYS.

Crown 8vo, Cloth Elegant, Gilt Top, 5/-.

The Voyage of the Avenger; OR, IN THE DAYS OF THE INQUISITION. By HENRY ST. JOHN, Author of "*A Middy of Nelson's Day*," &c. With Twenty-five Illustrations by PAUL HARDY.

In this new story by Mr. H. St. John, the reader is taken back to the days of "good queen Bess," and introduced to not a few of her most distinguished and adventurous subjects. As the sub-title indicates we have also glimpses of the cruel work of the Inquisition. The tale is full of incident, and should be a favourite with all those, old or young, who love the rapid succession of stirring adventure. The book is illustrated by Paul Hardy.

Crown 8vo, Cloth elegant.
2/-.

Geordie, the Black Prince.

By REV. J. M. RUSSELL, Author of "*The Flower Show of Fairley Court*," &c., &c. Illustrated by CAROLINE MANNING.

A story of North-country life, in which the hero, a boy of lowly origin overcomes difficulties, makes the most of opportunities, and eventually becomes what he has long aimed at becoming, a distinguished artist.

The book is especially adapted for Sunday School and Parish Libraries, as well as for a reward or prize book.

London: Jarrold and Sons, 10 and 11, Warwick Lane, E.C.
Of all Booksellers and at the Bookstalls.

BLACK BEAUTY.

THE AUTOBIOGRAPHY OF A HORSE.

120 *Entirely New Illustrations.* 4to, *Cloth Elegant,* 5/- *(Postage 4½d.)*

"Had the Society for the Prevention of Cruelty to Animals published this, we should say it had published its best work."—*Review.*

"It would be difficult to conceive one more admirably suited to its purpose." *Nonconformist.*

"The story is simply told and cleverly put together, and while it may be read with pleasure and profit by educated people, it is an excellent book to put into the hands of stable-boys, or any who have to do with horses." *Essex Standard.*

"As a book for young people it will be popular for its picturesque illustrations of all possible aspects of a horse's career." *Ipswich Journal.*

Of this book 180,000 have been printed in this country alone. It has also been very extensively reproduced in the United States, and Editions have been published in France and Italy.

The present 4to Edition has been produced at great expense. It contains 120 Illustrations by that eminent Artist, JOHN BEER, ESQ., facsimiled by the half-tone process, with beautiful results. It is artistically bound, and will no doubt be highly appreciated as a suitable gift book by many of the thousands who have been delighted with it in its cheaper form ; for as the Editor of *The Animal World* says, "The more often we have turned over the leaves of 'Black Beauty,' the greater has been our delight."

The Popular Editions at 2/-, 1 6, and 1/- are still on Sale.

London : Jarrold & Sons, 10 and 11, Warwick Lane, E.C.

Of all Booksellers and at the Bookstalls.

BEAUTIFUL JOE.

THE AUTOBIOGRAPHY OF A DOG.

BY MARSHALL SAUNDERS.

42nd Thousand. Illustrated. Popular Edition, Cloth, 2/-. Gilt Edges, 3/6.

The Countess of Aberdeen writes of the Canadian edition of "Beautiful Joe": "I am sure that all lovers of animals will welcome this book with eagerness as being eminently calculated to spread that knowledge and thought for dumb beasts which will lead to their humane treatment."

"The narrative is admirably conveyed and interesting from every point of view. If we had our wish and our way, the book should be in every school and in every house."—*The World.*

"The book is charmingly got up, and would make an excellent school-prize."—*British Weekly.*

"It is a capital story, and is certain to be popular among all lovers of animals." —*Sheffield Daily Telegraph.*

"For Sunday-school libraries and for reading alike in families, it is a most appropriate volume, sure to draw out the sympathies of young readers to their four-footed companions, and to teach them valuable lessons as to the right and kind treatment of dumb creatures."—*The Freeman.*

London: Jarrold and Sons, 10 and 11, Warwick Lane, E.C.
Of all Booksellers and at the Bookstalls.

Selections from Jarrolds' New Books.

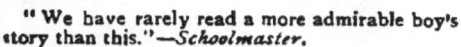

BOOKS OF ADVENTURE FOR BOYS.

Crown 8vo, Cloth. 3/6 each.

The Story Hunter. By

E. R. SUFFLING, Author of
"*Afloat in a Gipsy Van,*" "*Jethou,
or Crusoe Life in the Channel
Islands.*" Illustrated by PAUL
HARDY.

A volume so varied in its contents as
to please many tastes. Hypnotism is
the weapon which the Story Hunter
uses to bring down his quarry—uses,
too, with such effect that he is able to
present to the reader a collection of
thrilling narratives of the most hetero-
geneous character.

"The stories themselves purport to be a
collection formed by a gentleman who lives in
a caravan, journeys about the country, hypno-
tises likely subjects, and obtains from them,
when in that state, tales of remarkable events
that have happened to them. These tales are
all striking, and quite out of the ordinary line.
There is certainly no lack of imagination in
these tales."—*The Standard.*

"The stories are highly imaginative, and form a very interesting book."—*Essex Herald.*

"There is splendid stuff in this book for boys. Mr. Suffling knows how to thrill and
mystify."—*Cork Examiner.*

"They are certain to delight any boys who have a liking for the supernatural."—*Scotsman.*

"There are plenty of entertaining short tales in 'The Story Hunter.'"—*Graphic.*

"A very entertaining volume."—*Daily Chronicle.*

"A volume consisting of some ten stories, not one of which is weak or ineffective. We can
recommend the book as being a capital volume of literature."—*Observer.*

"'The Story Hunter' is an absorbing collection of tales, told by a gentleman who is in the
habit of travelling about the country in a caravan."—*Elizabethan.*

"The stories are well told, and will be acceptable to young people."—*Morning Post.*

"There is certainly no lack of imagination in these tales, and we predict that few who start
reading them will have done with the book until they reach the end of it."—*Devon and
Exeter Gazette.*

"Curious and fascinating are several of the stories. The book is nicely illustrated, and
would form a capital prize or present."—*Schoolmaster.*

"Nine or ten quaint tales, in which the supernatural plays a very important part."—*The
Gentlewoman.*

"The tales are well told, and full of interest."—*School Guardian.*

"Mr. Suffling knows parts of England well, and places his stories in scenes that will make
them enjoyable to readers of all ages." *Spectator.*

London: Jarrold and Sons, 10 and 11, Warwick Lane, E.C.

Of all Booksellers and at the Bookstalls.

Selections from Jarrolds' New Books.

Bob Strong's Holidays;

OR, ADRIFT IN THE CHANNEL.
By the Author of "*Afloat at Last,*"
"*The Wreck of the Nancy Bell,*"
&c. With Six Illustrations by JOHN
B. GREENE. 2nd Edition.

A bright, brisk, breezy book, breath-
ing out healthy ozone from every page;
full of incident and adventure, such
as will be liked and loved by every boy
and girl reader.

"Mr. Hutcheson, being so well-known as a
favourite writer for boys, the volume will, we are
sure, prove very popular. The book deals with
a cruise in the channel, and the adventures which
happened to Bob Strong during the cruise."—
Devon and Exeter Gazette.

"'Bob Strong's Holidays; or, Adrift in the Channel, by John C. Hutcheson, is the story of
the deadly peril of two youths of resources, who were cast adrift at sea in an open boat."—
Daily News.

"'Bob Strong's Holiday' is a perfect story for boys. It shows us how Bob Strong's
holiday is of a particularly adventurous order. He makes the acquaintance in the train, on
the way home from school, of Dick Allsop, who has run away from home and the tyranny of a
cruel step-father; and at Portsmouth, whither the boys are bound, they fall in with Captain
Dresser, and the adventures, which are the result of the friendship which springs up between
the three, are of a very interesting character, and are admirably related."—*Norfolk Chronicle*

"This healthy tale for boys, from the pen of Mr. Hutcheson, comes very opportunely. The
plot is extremely simple, and yet Mr. Hutcheson keeps up the interest of the reader in Bob
Strong in a wonderful manner. The book is attractive in appearance, and is a good presenta
tion work for boys."—*Cambridge Daily News.*

"It is a fine tale of the sea, full of thrilling situations, accompanied with a host of illustrations by Mr. John B. Greene."—*Book and News Trades' Gazette.*

"Another sterling sea story, that may safely be placed in any boy's hands. As a whole,
these are the most attractively-written and best illustrated volumes we have seen this season."
—*Board Teacher.*

"From Messrs. Jarrold and Sons, London, comes a tale for young readers, written by Mr.
John C. Hutcheson, and illustrated by J. B. Greene. It is a spirited and lively tale of the
adventures of a lad who got adrift at sea, although this is only the culmination of his 'larks,'
and might have been lost if it hadn't been for the fisher folk. Its title is 'Bob Strong's
Holidays,' and it is a capital book for a boy."—*The Scotsman.*

London: Jarrold and Sons, 10 and 11, Warwick Lane, E.C.
Of all Booksellers and at the Bookstalls.

Selections from Jarrolds' New Books.

Selections from Jarrolds' New Books.

OUR GIRLS' BOOKSHELF.

Crown 8vo, Cloth elegant. **3/6.**

Harum Scarum. By

ESMÈ STUART. Illustrated by E.
F. MANNING. 2nd Edition.

A bright, breezy story, full of life and
"go." The heroine is a young lady
from the bush, who suddenly finds herself the inmate of an English home distinguished for its stately propriety. The
atmosphere is not congenial, and over-
flowing spirits and masterful ways lead
to endless scrapes. The illustrations add
additional charm to a book already widely
popular.

"Miss Esmè Stuart has created a charming
character in 'Harum Scarum,' a tomboy of a
girl, who suddenly brought from the wilds of
Australia to the coldness and severity of the
house of an aristocratic relative in England,
turns it topsy-turvy, and wins the love of everybody by her goodness of heart and gaiety."—
The Star.

"A vivacious and life-like character sketch of a wilful untamed Australian girl. This girl
has a bright breezy nature and an indomitable will. An extremely amusing story, teeming
with natural and spontaneous fun that never for a moment degenerates into frivolous
buffoonery."—*Daily Telegraph.*

"There is a good deal of fascination in the whole story, by reason of its earnestness and
probability, and it deserves to enjoy extensive circulation."—*Belfast News Letter.*

"The tale is admirably told, and it is full of life and interest. A light satire on present-
day conventionalities is perceptible in the dialogue, which is for the most part clever and
natural."—*Dundee Advertiser.*

"Such as relish a bright breezy story told with unflagging vivacity should procure 'Harum
Scarum.' This is one of the brightest and in parts the merriest of recent novels."—*Publishers'
Circular.*

"There is an atmosphere of wholesome high spirits and natural kindness about the book,
which makes it refreshing to turn to after two or three novels full of social problems and
subtle characters. We recommend it to readers who look to novels for enlivenment rather
than for instruction or perplexity."—*Spectator.*

"A pleasant, simple story, brightly told and full of delightful touches of clever character-
painting, the life of the poor relation—who came from Australia to be educated by her
haughty relation, Lady Dove—will be welcomed by all who like to spend an idle hour or two
over something that is sweet, pure, and wholesome."—*Aberdeen Free Press.*

London: Jarrold and Sons, 10 and 11, Warwick Lane, E.C.
Of all Booksellers and at the Bookstalls.

Selections from Jarrolds' New Books.

ATTRACTIVE BOOKS FOR BOYS AND GIRLS.

Crown 8vo, Cloth, Illustrated. **3/6** *each.*

The Wild Ruthvens. By

CURTIS YORKE, Author of "*Dudley,*" "*Once,*" "*Hush!*" "*A Romance of Modern London,*" &c. Illustrated by E. F. MANNING. 5th Edition.

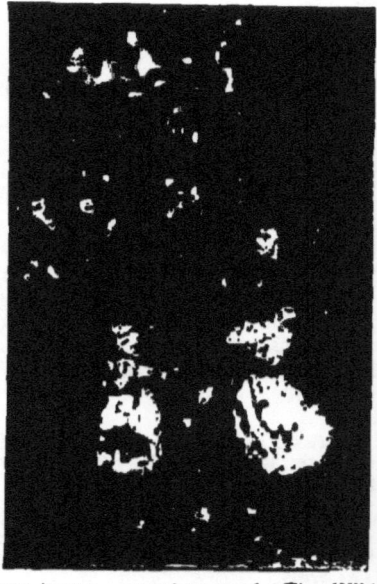

A story illustrating the mistakes, failures and successes of a family of unruly but warm-hearted boys and girls. They are ultimately softened and civilised by the influence of an invalid cousin, Dick Trevanion, who comes to live with them. He recovers, and, years later, marries the most rebellious and unruly (formerly) of all the family, Nancie Ruthven.

"An enchanting work. The story runs on with happy blithesome tread to the end, which is reached all too soon."—*St. Stephen's Review.*

"A most deserved popularity is that enjoyed by Curtis Yorke s capital story of 'The Wild Ruthvens,' which appeals to readers young and old alike. I advise anyone in search of a suitable book for a present not to choose before having a look at it."—*Hearth and Home.*

"The book is most amusing."—*Manchester Guardian.*

"Mr. Yorke has written here as good a boys' and girls' story as could be desired. The book is full of life and incident, and the moral is wholesome though not disagreeably obtruded There is an out-of-doors breeziness about the book to recommend it specially to young readers, and it has the additional charm of numerous and handsome illustrations."—*Dublin Freeman's Journal.*

"'The Wild Ruthvens' is a rattling, rollicking story of the daily life of a 'holy terror' of a family—they are not a bad lot at all, but undeniably humans of a vigorous nature, whose delight is in mischief, whose sorrow is in evil, and whose kindliness and true-heartedness brings them out triumphant in the end. The book should be exceedingly interesting to both boys and girls."—*Liberal Budget.*

"One naturally expects from this writer a wholly enjoyable story, and the nature expectation will not be disappointed in this case. 'The Wild Ruthvens' secured our interest at the outset, and retained it to the end."—*Glasgow Herald.*

"A lively book, full of the deeds of three mischievous lads. Schoolboys and their elders will find plenty to laugh at. Fun is here and there interspersed with deeds of pathos, that are an effective contrast to the wild behaviour of most of the members of a wild family."—*Manchester Evening News.*

London: Jarrold and Sons, 10 and 11, Warwick Lane, E.C.

Of all Booksellers and at the Bookstalls.

Selections from Jarrolds' New Books.

OUR GIRLS' BOOKSHELF.

Crown 8vo, Cloth elegant. 3/6.

Common Chords. By

RAYMOND JACBERNS, Author of "*An Uncut Diamond*," "*Witch Demima*." With Six Illustrations by ANNIE L. BEAL. 2nd Edition.

In "Common Chords" we have an admirable study of girl life in the present day. The heroine, anxious to get away from uncongenial surroundings, takes a situation as governess, and the story of her trials, discouragements, and successes is naturally and pleasingly told. The tone of the book is thoroughly pure and wholesome.

"This is a common-sense tale which touches the heart of the reader, and will, no doubt, become a favourite with girls who want to read something more than the ordinary 'love' story.' — *Book & News Trades Gazette.*

"Mr. Raymond Jacberns has written a story of unusual interest in which he displays considerable ability in characterization and in terseness and lucidity of expression."—*St. James' Gazette.*

"The authoress of 'An Uncut Diamond' and 'Mists' has put her very best work into the new book, with the only possible result. The characters are wondrously life-like in every way, and there is that homeliness about the whole which has distinguished all this writer's works."—*Western Daily Mercury.*

"We can assure our readers that they will not be disappointed when they introduce 'Common Chords' as a reward book. In our judgment there is no better girl's book in the market."—*Teachers' Aid.*

"The enjoyments and troubles of the youthful heroine are well narrated, and a tone of pleasant wholesomeness pervades the whole book. Girls will like this story for its simple unpretending aim and its vivid delineation of female character. Nice pictures and good printing make 'Common Chords' an excellent gift-book."—*Aberdeen Daily Free Press.*

"A pretty and interesting story about various girls and a young clergyman, written by Mr. Raymond Jacberns, and illustrated by Miss Annie L. Beal. It has a healthy interest of the study of gentle character, with a dash of mystery to keep the plot well together."—*The Scotsman.*

"'Common Chords' is admirably written, and is sure to command a ready acceptance on the part of the girls of the household."—*Eastern Daily Press.*

"Another story to interest and delight older girls is 'Common Chords.'"—*Hearth and Home.*

"One of those stories of strong domestic interest which Raymond Jacberns can tell so well."—*Birmingham Gazette.*

London: Jarrold & Sons, 10 and 11, Warwick Lane, E.C.

Of all Booksellers and at the Bookstalls.